Mr. Rabbit

Illustrated by
Oliver Lake

ISBN 978-0-9897814-6-6
Printed in Mexico on FSC® paper from well-managed forests
First printing November 2014, RR Donnelley, Reynosa

Music Together LLC
174 Nassau Street #340
Princeton NJ 08542
www.musictogether.com
(800) 728-2692

MUSIC TOGETHER®

Mr. Rabbit

Welcome

Since 1987, Music Together has been bringing the Joy of Family Music® to young children and their families. This Singalong Storybook offers a new way to enjoy one of our best-loved Music Together songs. We invite you to sing it, read it, and use it as a starting point for conversation and imaginative play with your child.

Using the Book

If you're a Music Together family, you might start singing as soon as you turn the pages. But even if you've never attended one of our classes, you and your child can have hours of fun and learning with this Singalong Storybook. Read the story and enjoy the illustrations with your child, and then try some of the suggested activities that follow. The book can also help inspire artwork or enhance pre-literacy skills. You can even invent your own variations of the story or involve the whole family in some musical dramatic play.

Using the Recording Of course, using the recording to learn the song will enhance your enjoyment of the book. See page 31 for ways to get the Singalong Storybook songs and see the video "Using Your Singalong Storybook Musically." Or, if you play an instrument such as piano or guitar, you'll find it easy to pick out the song using the music page at the end of the book.

Mister Rabbit, Mister Rabbit, your ear's mighty long!

Yes, my friend,
 they're put on wrong!

Every little soul must shine, shine, shine.

Every little soul must shine, shine, shine.

11

Mister Rabbit, Mister Rabbit, you've been in my cabbage patch.

Yes, my friend,
and I'm never
comin' back!

Every little soul must shine, shine, shine.
Every little soul must shine, shine, shine.

Mister Rabbit, Mister Rabbit, your tail's mighty white.

Yes, my friend,
and I'm gettin' out of sight!

Every little soul must shine, shine, shine.

Every little soul must shine, shine, shine. ㉓

Every little soul must shine, shine, shine.

Every little soul must shine, shine, shine.

Activities

Invent Verses

Make up your own verses about Mr. Rabbit—they don't have to rhyme. "Mr. Rabbit, Mr. Rabbit, your hat's mighty red. Yes, I know, it's covering my head." Or "...your feet are mighty big. Yes, I know, and I need to buy some shoes!"

Act It Out

Try acting out this song. Wag your finger at the naughty rabbit as you sing the first line; then make hopping bunny ears with your other hand as you sing the reply. Try giving each character different voices (low and high, stern and silly, loud and soft). Use puppets—or act out the parts with your child or another family member; then dance together on the "every little soul" chorus!

Animals

How many different animals can you find in your storybook? Try singing whole lines or verses on "meow," "woof," "quack," or "moo." Or make up new verses about some of the other animals. Ask your child for ideas and sing them out— don't worry about rhyming or making sense.

Discussion

Mr. Rabbit teaches us that different people "shine" in different ways. What does your child think it means to "shine"? Talk about the people you know and how their different gifts make your world brighter. Don't forget to include how your child shines!

Dance!

Put on the recording and have a hopping-fun dance with your child. It's okay to get a little silly: hop around, hold your hands to your head as rabbit ears, exaggerate your funkiest dance moves, be a back-up singer with an imaginary microphone. Your child will love singing and dancing with you— let your souls shine!

Mr. Rabbit

Traditional, arranged and
adapted by K. Guilmartin

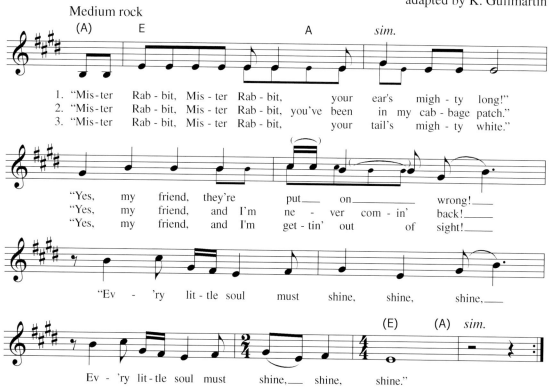

Medium rock

(A)   E   A   *sim.*

1. "Mis-ter   Rab-bit,   Mis-ter   Rab-bit,   your   ear's   migh-ty   long!"
2. "Mis-ter   Rab-bit,   Mis-ter   Rab-bit,   you've   been   in   my   cab-bage   patch."
3. "Mis-ter   Rab-bit,   Mis-ter   Rab-bit,   your   tail's   migh-ty   white."

"Yes,   my   friend,   they're   put___   on___   wrong!___
"Yes,   my   friend,   and   I'm   ne - ver   com-in'   back!___
"Yes,   my   friend,   and   I'm   get-tin'   out   of   sight!___

"Ev - 'ry   lit-tle   soul   must   shine,   shine,   shine,___

(E)   (A)   *sim.*

Ev - 'ry   lit-tle   soul   must   shine,___   shine,   shine."

About the Song

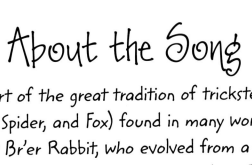

"Mr. Rabbit" is part of the great tradition of trickster heroes (including Coyote, Raven, Spider, and Fox) found in many world cultures. This song is most likely about Br'er Rabbit, who evolved from a mingling of Native American and African stories of the trickster Hare. In Music Together's adaptation of the popular folk song, our cunning rabbit gets out of perilous situations (in this case, being caught in a farmer's garden) with his quick wits and smooth talk, while sending us the message that—whatever our individual differences—we are all shining souls.

About Music Together®

Music Together classes offer a wide range of activities that are designed to be engaging and enjoyable for children from birth through age seven. By presenting a rich tonal and rhythmic mix as well as a variety of musical styles, Music Together provides children with a depth of experience that stimulates and supports their growing music skills and understanding.

Developed by Founder/Director Kenneth K. Guilmartin and his coauthor, Director of Research Lili M. Levinowitz, Ph.D., Music Together is built on the idea that all children are musical, that their parents and caregivers are a vital part of their music learning, and that their natural music abilities will flower and flourish when they are provided with a sufficiently rich learning environment.

And it's fun! Our proven methods not only help children learn to embrace and express their natural musicality—they often help their grateful grownups recapture a love of music, too. In Music Together classes all over the world, children and their families learn that music can happen anywhere, every day, at any time of the day—and they learn they can make it themselves.

Known worldwide for our mixed-age family classes, we have also adapted our curriculum to suit the needs of infants, older children, and children in school settings such as preschools, kindergartens, and early elementary grades. Visit www.musictogether.com to see video clips of Music Together classes; read about the research behind the program; purchase instruments, CDs, and books; and find a class near you. Keep singing!

Getting the Music

There is a download card for the song "Mr. Rabbit" in the front of this book; or at www.musictogether.com/storybooks you can listen to the song anytime. You can also find it on the award-winning Music Together CD **Family Favorites® 2.** CDs and downloads are available from Music Together, iTunes, and Amazon. To get the most out of your storybook, see the video **"Using Your Singalong Storybook Musically"** on our website.

The Family Favorites® 2 CD includes 19 songs and a 32-page booklet with many family activities to enjoy.

Come visit us at **www.musictogether.com.**

Music Together LLC

Kenneth K. Guilmartin, Founder/Director

Catherine Judd Hirsch, Director of Publishing and Marketing

Marcel Chouteau, Manager of Production and Distribution

Jill Bronson, Manager of Retail and Market Research

Susan Pujdak Hoffman, Senior Editor

Kate Battenfeld, Devi Borton, Linda Brasaemle, Contributing Writers

Developed by Q2A/Bill Smith, New York, NY